FATHER! FATHER! BURNING BRIGHT

The hospital rang the school to say Mr. Midgley's father was dying. The timing was good. Only Midgley's father would have managed to stage his farewell in the middle of *Meet the Parents* week.

Alan Bennett first appeared on the stage in *Beyond the Fringe*. His stage plays include *Forty Years On*, *Habeas Corpus*, *Enjoy* and *Kafka's Dick*, and his adaptation of *The Wind in the Willows* and *The Madness of George III* were both presented at The Royal National Theatre. He has written many television plays, notably *An Englishman Abroad* and the *Talking Heads* monologues. *The Lady in the Van*, which originally appeared in the *London Review of Books* in 1989 and was then published by Profile Books, has recently been adapted for the stage. *Writing Home*, a collection of diaries and prose, came out in 1994 and his first story, *The Clothes They Stood Up In*, was published in 1998.

FATHER! FATHER!

BURNING BRIGHT

ALAN BENNETT

P

PROFILE BOOKS

in association with

LONDON REVIEW OF BOOKS

First published in book form
in Great Britain in 2000 by
PROFILE BOOKS LTD
58a Hatton Garden, London EC1N 8LX
www.profilebooks.co.uk

Previously published in 2000 by
LONDON REVIEW OF BOOKS
28 Little Russell Street, London WC1A 2HN
www.lrb.co.uk

Typeset in Quadraat
Cover and text design by Peter Campbell
Printed and bound in Great Britain by
St Edmundsbury Press, Bury St Edmunds

Author photograph © John Timbers

A CIP catalogue record for this book is available
from the British Library.

ISBN 1 86197 203 2

FATHER! FATHER!

BURNING BRIGHT

Father! Father! Burning Bright was the original title of a BBC television film I wrote in 1982 but which was subsequently entitled *Intensive Care*. The main part, Midgley, had been hard to cast, though when I was writing the script I thought it was a role I might play myself until, that is, I got to the scene where Midgley goes to bed with Valery, the slatternly nurse. That, I thought, effectively ruled me out as I didn't fancy having to take my clothes off under the bored appraisal of an entire film crew.

Not that it would have been the first time. Back in 1966 I was acting in a BBC TV comedy series I had written which included a weekly spot, 'Life and Times in NW1', in one episode of which I was supposedly in bed with a neighbour's wife. The scene was due to be shot in the studio immediately after a tea break, and rather than brave the scrutiny of the TV crew, I thought that during the break I might sneak on to the set and be already in bed when the crew returned. So I tiptoed into the studio in my underpants, failing to notice that a lighting rig had been positioned behind the bedroom door. When I opened it there was an almighty crash, the lights came down and everybody rushed into the studio to find me sprawled in my underpants among the wreckage and subject to a far more searching and hostile scrutiny than would otherwise have been the case. No more bedroom scenes for me, I thought.

However, the role of Midgley proved hard to cast and after a lot of toing and froing, including what was virtually an audition, I found myself playing the part. Like some other leading roles that I have written, it verged on the anonymous, all the fun and jokes put into the mouths of the supporting characters while Midgley, whom the play is supposed to be about, never managed to be much more than morose.

It was in the hope of finding more to the character than this that I decided, before the shooting started, to write the story up in prose. When I'd finished I showed it to the director in the hope that it might help him to appreciate what the screenplay was about. He received it politely enough and in due course gave me it back, I suspect without having read it, directors tending to form their own ideas about a text, one script from the author hard enough to cope with without wanting two.

So I put it away in a drawer in 1982 where it has remained ever since. I've dusted it off and published it now, I suppose, as part of an effort to slim down my *Nachlass* and generally tidy up.

On the many occasions Midgley had killed his father, death had always come easily. He died promptly, painlessly and without a struggle. Looking back, Midgley could see that even in these imagined deaths he had failed his father. It was not like him to die like that. Nor did he.

The timing was good, Midgley acknowledged that. Only his father would have managed to stage his farewell in the middle of a 'Meet The Parents' week. It was not a function Midgley enjoyed. Each year he was dismayed how young the parents had grown, the youth of fathers in particular. Most sported at least one tattoo, with ears and noses now routinely studded. Midgley saw where so many of his pupils got it from. One father wore a swastika necklace, of the sort Midgley had wondered if he felt justified in confiscating from a boy. And a mother he had talked to had had green hair. 'Not just green,' muttered Miss

Tunstall, 'bright green. And then you wonder the girls get pregnant.'

That was the real point of these get-togethers. The teachers were appalled by the parents but found their shortcomings reassuring. With parents like these, they reasoned, who could blame the schools? The parents, recalling their own teachers as figures of dignity and authority, found the staff sloppy. Awe never entered into it, apparently. 'Too human by half' was their verdict. So both Nature and Nurture came away, if not satisfied, at any rate absolved. 'Do you wonder?' said the teachers, looking at the parents. 'They get it at school,' said the parents.

'Coretta's bin havin' these massive monthlies. Believe me, Mr Midgley, I en never seen menstruatin' like it.' Mrs Azakwale was explaining her daughter's poor showing in Use of English. 'She bin wadin' about in blood to her ankles, Mr Midgley. I en never out of the launderette.' Behind Mrs Azakwale, Mr Horsfall listened openly and with unconcealed scepticism, shaking his head slowly as Midgley caught his eye. Behind Mr Horsfall,

Mr Patel beamed with embarrassment as the large black woman said these terrible things so loudly. And beyond Mr Patel, Midgley saw the chairs were empty.

Mrs Azakwale took Coretta's bloodstained track-record over to the queue marked Computer Sciences, leaving Midgley faced with Mr Horsfall and Martin.

Mr Horsfall did not dye his hair nor wear an earring. His hair was now fashionably short but only because he had never got round to wearing it fashionably long. Nor had his son Martin ever ventured under the drier; his ears, too, were intact. Mr Horsfall was a detective sergeant.

'I teach Martin English, Mr Horsfall,' said Midgley, wishing he had not written 'Hopeless' on Martin's report, a document now gripped by Mr Horsfall in his terrible policeman's hand.

'Martin? Is that what you call him?'

'But that's his name.' Midgley had a moment of wild anxiety that it wasn't, that the father would accuse him of not even knowing the name of his son.

'His name's Horsfall. Martin is what we call him, his mother and me. For your purposes I should have thought his name was Horsfall. Are you married?'

'Yes.'

Horsfall was not impressed. He had spent long vigils in public toilets as a young constable. Many of the patrons had turned out to be married and some of them teachers. Marriage involved no medical examination, no questionnaire to speak of. Marriage for these people was just the bush they hid behind.

'What does my son call you?'

'He calls me Mr Midgley.'

'Doesn't he call you sir?'

'On occasion.'

'Schools . . .' Horsfall sniffed.

His son ought to have been small, nervous and bright, Midgley the understanding schoolteacher taking his part against his big, overbearing parent. He would have put books into his hands, watched him flower so that in time to come the boy would look back and think 'Had it not been for him . . .' Such myths sustained Midgley when he woke in the small hours of the morning and drowsed during the middle period of the afternoon. But they were myths. Martin was large and dull. He was not unhappy. He would not flower. He was not even embarrassed. He was probably on his father's side, thought Midgley, as he sat there looking at his large inherited hands, and occasionally picked at one of a scattering of violet-painted warts.

'What worries me,' said Horsfall, 'is that he can scarcely put two words together.'

This was particularly hurtful to a man who, in his professional capacity, specialised in converting the faltering confessions of semi-illiterates into his plain policeman's prose. He could do it. At four o'clock in the morning after a day spent combing copses and dragging ponds, never mind house-to-house enquiries, he could do it. Why not his son?

'You show me up, Martin, having to come along here. I don't grudge coming along here. But what I would like to have come along here as is a proud father. To be told of your achievements. Be shown your name in gilt letters on the honours board. Martin Horsfall. But no. What is it? It's Geography: Poor. History: Poor. English: Hopeless. PE: Only fair.' Why Martin?'

'Why Mr Midgley? And why hopeless? Geography: Poor. History: Poor. English: Hopeless. Is he hopeless or are you?'

'He doesn't try.'

'Do you challenge him? We challenge him at home. His mother and I challenge him. Does he get challenged at school? I don't see it.' Horsfall looked round but caught the eye of Mr Patel, who was smiling in anticipation of his interview. Mr Patel's son was clever. Blacks, Indians. That was why. Challenge. How could there be any challenge?

'I never had chances like he had. And I dare say you didn't. We never had chances like that, Martin.'

At the 'we' Midgley flinched, suddenly finding himself handcuffed to Horsfall in the same personal pronoun.

'A school like this. Modern buildings. Light. Air. Sporting facilities tip-top. Volleyball. If somebody had come up to me when I was your age and said "There are facilities for volleyball", I would have gone down on my knees. What do you say?'

The question Horsfall was asking his son had no obvious answer. Indeed, it was not really a question at all. 'Justify your life'; that was what this dull and dirty youth was being asked to do. Not seeing that justification was necessary, the son was silent and the father waited.

And it was in the middle of this silence that Miss Tunstall came up to say the hospital had telephoned. Except that, sensing this was not simply a silence but an essential part of what was being said, she did not immediately interrupt but made little wavings with her hand behind Mr Horsfall's head, who – a policeman and ever on the watch for mockery – turned round. So it was to him that Miss Tunstall gave the bad news (a man in any case used to transactions with ambulances, hospitals and all the regimes of crisis).

'The hospital's just rung. Mr Midgley's father's been taken ill.' And only then, having delivered her message did she look at Midgley, who thus heard his father was dying at second-hand and then only as a kind of apology.

'They're ringing the ward,' said Midgley. 'It's a fall, apparently.' One ear was in Miss Tunstall's office, the other fifty miles away in some nowhere behind a switchboard.

'You want to pray it's not his hip,' said Miss Tunstall. 'That's generally the weak spot.' She had a mother of her own. 'The pelvis heals in no time, surprisingly.' She did not sound surprised. Her mother had broken her pelvis and she had thought it was the beginning of the end. 'No. It's when it's the hip it's complicated.'

'Switchboard's on the blink,' said a voice.

'Join the club,' said another. 'I've been on the blink all day.'

'It's the dreaded lurgi,' said the first voice.

'Hello,' said Midgley. But there was silence.

'She took a nasty tumble in Safeway's last week,' went on Miss Tunstall. 'They do when they get older. It's what you must expect.' She expected it all the time. 'Their bones get brittle.'

She cracked her fingers and adjusted the spacing.

'Maintenance,' said a new voice.

'I've been wrongly connected,' said Midgley.

'It's these ancillary workers,' said Miss Tunstall. 'Holding the country to ransom. Other people's suffering is their bread and butter.' She was wanting to get on with a notice about some boys acting the goat in the swimming baths but felt she ought to wait until Midgley had heard one way or the other. Her mother was 82. The last twenty years had not been easy and had she known what was in store she thought now she would probably have stabbed her mother to death the second she turned 60. These days it would only have meant a suspended sentence or if the worst came to the worst open prison. Miss Tunstall had once been round such an institution with the school and found it not uncongenial. A picnic in fact.

'Records are on the warpath again,' said a

voice in Midgley's ear.

'It never rains,' said another.

'Should I be sterilisin' this?' said a black voice.

'Search me, dear,' said an emancipated one.

'Hello,' said Midgley. 'HELLO.'

Softly Miss Tunstall began to type.

Midgley thought of his father lying in bed, dying but not wanting to be any trouble.

'No joy?' said Miss Tunstall, uncertain whether it would be better to underline 'the likelihood of a serious accident'. 'And then they wonder why people are stampeding to BUPA.'

Midgley decided he had been forgotten then a crisp voice suddenly said 'Sister Tudor'.

'I'm calling about a patient, a Mr Midgley.'

Noiselessly Miss Tunstall added an exclamation mark to 'This hooliganism must now STOP!' and waited, her hands spread over the keys.

'What is the patient's name?'

'Midgley,' said Midgley. 'He came in this morning.'

'When was he admitted?'

'This morning.'

'Midgley.' There was a pause. 'We have no Midgley. No Midgley has been admitted here. Are you sure you have the right ward?'

'He was admitted this morning. I was told he was seriously ill.'

'Oh yes.' Her tone changed. 'Midgley. What is your name?'

'Midgley.'

'Are you next of kin?'

'My father is dead,' he thought. 'Only the dead have next of kin.'

'I'm his son.'

Miss Tunstall folded her hands in her lap.

'He's not at all well.' The tone was reproachful rather than sympathetic. 'We think he's had a stroke. He's been lying on the floor. He ought to have been in hospital sooner. There's now the question of pneumonia. It's touch and go.'

'It's touch and go,' said Midgley, putting the phone down.

'How old is he?' said Miss Tunstall, noticing she had typed 'tooling' for 'fooling'.

'He's 74.'

Her mother was 82. She ripped out the paper and wound in another sheet. Life was unfair.

The door opened.

'Been on the phone again Midgley?' said the headmaster. 'I'm the one who has to go cap in hand to the Finance Committee.'

'Mr Midgley's father's ill,' said Miss Tunstall, once again the apologetic herald. 'Apparently it's touch and go.'

And she started typing like the wind.

'Of course you can go. Of course you must go. One's father. There can be no question. A filial obligation.' Midgley was in the headmaster's study. 'It's awkward, of course. But then it always is.' It was death. It was a reshuffling of the timetable.

Midgley's thoughts were with his father in Intensive Care.

'Was he getting on in years?'

No effort was being spared to keep him alive and in the present and yet grammatically he kept slipping into the past.

'He's 74.'

'Seventy-four. Once upon a time I thought that was old. You won't be gone long? What, three, four days?' In his mind the headmaster roughed out a timetable whereby Midgley senior could decently die, be buried and Midgley junior be back in harness. Radical surgery on the timetable might still be avoided.

'Let me see. It's English, Integrated Humanities and Creative Arts, nothing else, is there?'

'Environmental Studies.'

The headmaster groaned. 'That's the awkward one. Pilbeam's off on another course. That's the trouble with the environment, it involves going on courses. I'll be glad when the environment is confined to the textbooks.'

'Ah well,' said the headmaster. 'It can't be helped.' He had never understood the fuss people made about their parents. 'Both of mine were despatched years ago. A flying bomb.' He made it sound like a victory for common sense.

'He must have fallen and not been able to get up,' said Midgley. 'He was lying there two days.'

'An all too familiar scenario these days,' said

the headmaster. 'Isolated within the community. Alone in the crowd. You must not feel guilty.'

'I generally go over at weekends,' said Midgley.

'It will give Tomlinson an opportunity to do some of his weird and wonderful permutations with the timetable. Though I fear this one will tax even Tomlinson's talents.'

The headmaster opened the door.

'One must hope it is not as grave as it appears. One must hope he turns the corner. Corners seem to have gone out of medicine nowadays. In the old days the sick were always turning them. Illness is now much more of a straight road. Why is that?'

It was not a question he wanted answering.

'Antibiotics?' said Midgley, lingering.

'Sometimes one has the impression modern medicine encourages patients to loiter.' It was Midgley who was taking his time.

'Mistakenly, one feels. God speed.'

Miss Tunstall had finished the notice about acting the goat in the swimming baths and the headmaster now glanced through it, taking out his pen. She made a start on another notice about the bringing of pupils' cars to school, one of the head's 'privilege not a right' notices. Midgley still hesitated.

'I'm not sure if we've couched this in strong enough terms, Daphne.'

'It's as you dictated it.'

'I have no doubt. But I feel more strongly about it now. Nothing else is there, Midgley?'

Midgley shook his head and went out.

'A boy slips. Is pushed and we are talking about concussion. A broken neck. A fatality, Daphne. I intend to nail the culprits. I want them to know they will be crucified.'

'Shall I put that?'

The headmaster looked at her sharply and wondered if Miss Tunstall was through the menopause.

'We must find a paraphrase. But first the problems caused by this business of Midgley père. Ask Tomlinson to step over will you, Daphne. Tell him to bring his coloured pencils. And a rubber.'

'Tomato or my jam?'

'Tomato.'

The hospital was fifty miles away. His wife was making him sandwiches. He sat in his raincoat at the kitchen table, watching her apply a faint smear of Flora to the wholemeal bread.

'I wanted to go over this last weekend,' said Midgley. 'I would have gone over if your Margaret hadn't suddenly descended.'

'You knew they were coming. They'd been coming for weeks. It's one of the few things Mother's got to look forward to.' Mrs Midgley's mother was stood staring out of the window. 'Don't blame our Margaret.'

'I just never expected it,' said Midgley.

If you expected something it didn't happen.

'I expected it,' said his wife, putting on a shiny plastic apron emblazoned with a portrait of Sylvia Plath.

'I expected it. Last time I went over he came to the door to wave me off. He's never done that before. Bless him.' She slipped on a pair of padded

Union Jack mittens and sinking to her knees before the oven gave the Shift a trial blast. 'I think people know.'

'He does come to the door,' said Midgley. 'He always comes to the door.' And it was true he did, but only, Midgley felt, to show that the visit had been so short it needed extending. Though once, catching sight of him in the rear-view mirror, waving, Midgley had cried.

'He was trying to tell me something,' said his wife. 'I know a farewell when I see one.' A fine spray misted the oven's pale grey walls. 'Shouldn't you be going?'

'Is it Saturday today?' said her mother.

Ten minutes later Midgley was sitting on the stairs and his wife had started hoovering.

'I'm not going to let him down. I want to be there when he goes,' shouted Midgley.

The vacuum was switched off.

'What?'

'He loved me.'

'I can't think why,' said Midgley's wife. 'It's not as if you take after him,' and she switched on again, 'not one little bit.'

'Joyce,' her mother called, 'when is that chiropodist coming?'

Midgley looked at his watch. It was three o'clock. At ten past Mrs Midgley took to dusting. It was always assumed the housework put her in a bad temper. The truth was if she was in a bad temper she did the housework. So it came to the same thing.

'He had strength,' she said, dusting a group of lemonade bottles of various ages. 'Our Colin is going to be strong. He loved Colin.'

'Does he know?' asked Midgley.

'Yes. Only it hasn't hit him yet.'

Hoarse shouting and a rhythmic drumming on the floor indicated that his son was seeking solace in music.

'When it does hit him,' said his mother, picking at a spot of rust on a recently acquired Oxo tin, 'he is going to be genuinely heartbroken. There's always a gap. It was on *Woman's Hour*. Poor old Frank.'

'I've never understood,' said Midgley, 'why

you call him Frank. He's my father.'

She looked at the 1953 Coronation mug, wondering if it was altogether too recent an artefact to have on display.

'He has a name. Frank is his name.'

It was not only the date, the Coronation mug was about the only object in the house Midgley had contributed to the decor, having been issued with it in 1953 when he was at primary school.

'I call him Dad,' said Midgley.

'He's not Dad, is he? Not my dad, I call him Frank because that's the name of a person. To me he is a person. That's why we get on.'

She was about to hide the mug behind a cast-iron money-box in the shape of a grinning black man then thought better of it. They had too many things. And there would be more coming from his dad. She cheered up slightly.

Her husband kissed her and opened the back door.

'It isn't though,' he said.

'It isn't what?'

'Why you get on. Treating him like a person.'

Seeing her stood there in her silly apron he felt sorry for her, and wished he had kept quiet.

'You get on,' he said (and because he was sorry for her tried to make it sound as if she was justified), 'you get on because you both despise me.'

'Listen.' She brought him away from the door and closed it. Mrs Barnes next door, who had once described their marriage as uninhibited, was putting out a few opportune clothes. 'Your father is 74. He is dying. Considering the time you've been hanging about here he is possibly already dead yet you resent the fact that he and I were friends. I seem to have married someone very low down in the evolutionary chain. You might want one or two tissues.' And she darted at him and thrust them into his pocket.

Midgley opened the door again.

'It's just that when you and he were together I didn't exist.'

'I am married,' she shouted, 'to the cupboard under the sink.' A remark made more mysterious to Mrs Barnes by the sound of a passing ice-cream van playing the opening bars of the 'Blue

Danube'.

'He is *dying*, Denis. Will you exist now? Will that satisfy you?' She was crying.

'I'll make it right, Joyce,' said Midgley. 'I'll be there when he goes. I'll hold his hand.'

He held hers, still in their Union Jack mittens. 'If I let him down now he'd stay with me the rest of my life. I did love him, Joyce.'

'I *want* him to stay with you the rest of your life. That's what I want. I think of his kindness. His unselfishness. His unflagging courtesy. The only incredible thing is that someone so truly saintly should have produced such a pill of a son.'

She took off Sylvia Plath and hung her behind the door. She had stopped crying.

'But I suppose that's your mother.'

'Shut up about my mother,' said Midgley.

His mother was a sore point. 'My mother is dead.'

'So is your father by now probably. Go!'

Midgley took her by the shoulders.

'Things will change then, you'll see. I'll change. I'll be a different person. I can . . . go.

Live! Start!' He kissed her quickly and warmly and ran from the door down the little drive towards the van. His wife rushed to the door to catch him.

'Start?' she shouted. 'Start what? You're 39.'

'They had another do today,' Mrs Barnes told her husband that evening. 'It doesn't say much for a university education.'

Coming off the Leeds and Bradford Ring Road Midgley stopped at a zebra to let an old man cross. The old man held up a warning hand, and slowly moved across, glowering at the car. Midgley revved his engine and the old man stopped, glared and went on with seemingly deliberate slowness. Someone behind hooted. Midgley did not wait for the old man to reach the kerb but drove off with a jerk. Glancing in his mirror Midgley saw the old man slip and nearly fall.

At the hospital the first person he saw was Aunty Kitty, his father's sister. She said nothing, kissing him wordlessly, her eyes closed to indicate her grief lay temporarily beyond speech. The scene played she took his arm (something he disliked) and they followed the signs to Intensive Care.

'I thought you'd have been here a bit since,' said his Aunty. 'I've been here since two o'clock. You'll notice a big change.' They were going down a long featureless corridor. 'He's not like my brother. He's not the Frank I knew.' Visitors clustered at the doors of wards, waiting their turn to sit beside the beds of loved ones. Aunty Kitty favoured them with a brave smile. 'I don't dislike this colour scheme,' she said. 'I've always liked oatmeal. His doctor's black.'

Intensive Care had a waiting room to itself, presumably, Midgley thought, for the display of Intensive Grief, and there was a woman crying in the corner. 'Her hubby's on the critical list,' mouthed Aunty Kitty. 'Their eldest girl works for Johnson and Johnson. They'd just got back from Barbados. The nurse is white but she's not above eighteen.' The nurse came in. 'This is my nephew,' said Aunty Kitty. 'Mr Midgley's son. Your father's got a room to himself, love.'

'They all do,' said the nurse, 'at this stage.'

Midgley's father lay propped up against the pillows, staring straight ahead through the window at a blank yellow wall. His arms lay outside the coverlet, palms upward as if accepting his plight and awaiting some sort of deliverance. They had put him into some green hospital pyjamas, with half-length sleeves the functionalism of which seemed too modish to Midgley, who had only ever seen his father in bed in striped pyjamas, or sometimes his shirt. The garment was open and a monitor clung to his chest, and above the bed the television screen blipped steady and regular. Midgley watched it for a moment.

'Dad,' he said to himself.

'Dad. It's me, Denis.'

He put himself between the bed and the window so that if his father could see he would know he was there. He had read that stroke victims were never unconscious, just held incommunicado. 'In the most solitary confinement,' the article had said, the writer himself a doctor and too much taken with metaphor.

'It's all right, Dad.'

He took a chair and sat halfway down the bed, putting his hand over his father's inert palm.

His father looked well in the face, which was ruddy and worn, the skin of his neck giving way sharply to the white of his body. The division between his known head and the unknown body had shocked Midgley when he had first seen it as a child, when his Dad took him swimming at the local baths. It was still the same. He had never sat in the sun all his life.

'I'm sorry, Dad,' said Midgley.

'Are you next of kin?' It was another nurse.

'Son.'

'Not too long then.'

'Is the doctor around?'

'Why? What do you want to know? There's nothing wrong, is there? No complaints?'

'I want to know how he is.'

'He's very poorly. You can see.'

She looked down at her left breast and lifted a watch.

'Doctor'll be round in about an hour. He's very busy.'

'I wonder where he is,' said Aunty Kitty.

'She said he was busy.'

They were back in the waiting room.

Aunty Kitty looked at him with what he imagined she imagined was a look of infinite sadness, mingled with pity ('Sorrow and love flow mingling down' came into his mind from the hymn). 'Not the doctor, your dad, love. Behind that stare he's somewhere, wandering. You know,' she said vaguely, 'in his mind. Where is he?'

She patted his hand.

'I don't suppose with having been to university you believe in an after-life. That's always the first casualty.'

For a while she read the small print on her pension book and Midgley thought about his childhood. Nurses came and went, leading their own lives and a man wiped plastic-covered mattresses in the corridor. Every time a nurse came near he made remarks like 'It's all right for some' or 'No rest for the wicked.' Once the matron glided silently by, majestic and serene on her electric trolley. 'They're a new departure,' said Aunty

Kitty. 'I could do with one of those. I'll just pop and have another peep at your dad.'

'What does that look on his face mean?' she said when she came back. Midgley thought it meant he should have gone over to see him last Sunday. It meant that his dad had been right about him all along and now he was dying and whose fault was that? That was what it meant. 'This unit was opened by the Duchess of Kent,' said Aunty Kitty. 'They have a tip-top kidney department.'

The fascinations of medicine and royalty were equal in Aunty Kitty's mind and whenever poss-ible she found a connection between the two. Had she been told she was dying but from the same disease as a member of the Royal Family she would have died happy.

'There's some waiting done in hospitals,' she said presently. 'Ninety per cent of it's waiting. Would you call this room oatmeal or cream?'

A young man came through, crying.

'His wife was in an accident,' Aunty Kitty ex-plained. 'One of those head-on crashes. The car was a write-off. Did you come in your van?'

Midgley nodded.

'You'll be one of these two-car families, then? Would you say she was black?' A Thai nurse looked in briefly and went out again. 'You don't see that many of them. She's happen a refugee.'

Midgley looked at his watch. It was an hour since he had spoken to the nurse. He went in and stood at the desk but there was no one about. He stood at the door of his father's room. He had not moved, his unseeing eyes fixed on a window-cleaner, who with professional discretion carefully avoided their gaze.

'I always thought I'd be the first to go,' said Aunty Kitty, looking at an advertisement in *Country Life*. 'Fancy. Two swimming pools. I could do without two swimming pools. When you get to my age you just want somewhere you can get round nicely with the hoover. They've never got to the bottom of my complaint. They lowered a microscope down my throat but there was nothing. I wouldn't live in Portugal if they paid me. Minstrels' gallery, I shouldn't know what to do with a minstrels' gallery if I had one. Mr Penry-Jones wanted to put me on this machine the Duke of Gloucester inaugurated. This body-scan thing. Only there was such a long waiting-list apparently.'

A nurse came through.

'She's the one I was telling you about. I asked her if your dad was in a coma or just unconscious. She didn't know. They're taking them too young these days.'

'Aunty,' said Midgley.

'It isn't as if she was black. Black you don't expect them to know.'

'What was my dad like?'

Aunty Kitty thought for a moment.

'He never had a wrong word for anybody. He'd do anybody a good turn. Shovel their snow. Fetch their coal in. He was that type. He was a saint. You take after your mother more.'

'I feel I lack his sterling qualities,' said Midgley some time later. 'Grit. Patience. Virtues bred out of adversity.'

'You wouldn't think they'd have curtains in a

hospital, would you?' said Aunty Kitty. 'You wouldn't think curtains would be hygienic. I'm not keen on purple anyway.'

'Deprivation for instance,' said Midgley.

'What?'

'I was never deprived. That way he deprived me. Do you understand?'

'I should have gone to secondary school,' she said. 'I left at thirteen, same as your dad.'

'I know I had it easier than he did,' said Midgley. 'But I was grateful. I didn't take it for granted.'

'You used to look bonny in your blazer.'

'It isn't particularly enjoyable, education.' Midgley had his head in his hands. 'I had what he wanted. Why should that be enjoyable?'

'Mark's got his bronze medal,' said Aunty Kitty. 'Did you not ought to be ringing round?'

'About the bronze medal?'

'About your dad.'

'I'll wait till I've seen the doctor.'

It was half-past six.

'They go on about these silicon chips, you'd

think they'd get all these complaints licked first, somebody's got their priorities wrong. Then he's always been a right keen smoker has Frank. Now he's paying the price.'

Midgley fell asleep.

'Robert Donat had bronchitis,' said Aunty Kitty.

'Mr Midgley.' The doctor shook his shoulder.

'Denis,' said Aunt Kitty, 'it's doctor.'

He was a pale young Pakistani, and for a moment Midgley thought he had fallen asleep in class and was being woken by a pupil.

'Mr Midgley?' He was grave and precise, 26 at the most.

'Your father has had a stroke.' He looked at his clipboard. 'How severe it is hard to tell. When he was brought in he was suffering from hypothermia.'

Aunt Kitty gave a faint cry. It was a scourge that had been much in the news.

'He must have fallen and been lying there, two days at least.'

'I generally go over at weekends,' said Midgley.

'Pneumonia has set in. His heart is not strong. All things considered,' he looked at the clipboard again, 'we do not think he will last the night.'

As he went away he tucked the clipboard under his arm and Midgley saw there was nothing on it.

'Only three phones and two of them duff. You wouldn't credit it,' said a fat man. 'Say you were on standby for a transplant. It'd be just the same.' He jingled his coins and a young man in glasses on the working phone put his head outside the helmet.

'I've one or two calls to make,' he said cheerfully.

'Oh hell,' said the fat man.

'There's a phone outside physio. Try there,' said a passing nurse.

'I'll try there,' said the fat man.

Midgley sat on.

'Hello,' said the young man brightly. 'Dorothy? You're a grandma.' He looked at Midgley while he was talking, but without seeing him.

'A grandma,' he shouted. 'Yes!' There was a pause. 'Guess,' said the young man and listened. 'No,' he said. 'Girl. Seven and a half pounds. 5.35. Both doing well. I'm ringing everybody. Bye, Grandma.'

Midgley half rose as the young man put the receiver back, but sat back as he consulted a bit of paper then picked it up again and dialled.

'Hello, Neil. Hi. You're an uncle . . . You're an uncle. Today. Just now. 5.35. Well, guess.' He waited. 'No. Girl. No. I'm over the moon. So you can tell Christine she's an aunty. Yes, a little cousin for Josephine. How's it feel to be an uncle? . . . Bye.'

Midgley got up and stood waiting. The young man took another coin and dialled again. It was a way of breaking news that could be adapted for exits as well as entrances, thought Midgley.

'Hello, Margaret. You're a widow. A widow . . . This afternoon. Half-past two . . . How's it feel to be bereaved?'

'Betty,' said the young man. 'Congratulations.

You're an aunty. Aunty Betty. I won't ask you to guess,' he went on hurriedly. 'It's a girl. Susan's over the moon. And I am.'

With each call his enthusiasm had definitely decreased. Midgley reflected that this baby was well on the way to being a bore and it was only a couple of hours old.

'I'm just telephoning with the glad tidings. Bye, Aunty.'

The proud father put a new pile of coins on the box and Midgley was moved to intervene.

'Could I just make one call?'

'Won't it wait,' said the young man. 'I was here first. I'm a father.'

'I'm a son,' said Midgley. 'My father's dying.'

'There's no need to take that tone,' said the young man, stepping out of the helmet. 'You should have spoken up. There's a phone outside physio.'

Midgley listened to the phone ringing along the passage at his father's brother's house.

'Uncle Ernest? It's Denis. Dad's been taken poorly.'

'You mean Frank?' said his uncle.

'Yes. Dad. He's had a stroke,' said Midgley. 'And a fall. And now he's got pneumonia.' Somehow he felt he ought to have selected two out of three, not laid everything on the line first go off.

'Oh dear, oh dear, oh dear,' said his uncle. 'Our Frank.'

'Can you ring round and tell anybody who might want to come. The doctor says he won't last the night.'

'From here? Me ring?'

It started pipping.

'Yes. I'm in a box. There are people waiting.'

'You never know,' said the young man. 'They can work miracles nowadays.'

'This is what I'd call an industrial lift,' said Uncle Ernest, tapping the wall with his strong boot. 'It's not an ordinary passenger lift, this. It's as big as our sitting room.'

It stopped and a porter slid a trolley in beside Midgley. A woman looked up at him and smiled faintly.

'Is it working?' said the porter. The little head closed its eyes.

'We've just had a nice jab and now we're going for a ta ta.'

Behind a glass panel Midgley watched the concrete floors pass.

'It's very solidly constructed,' said Uncle Ernest, looking at the floor. 'These are overlapping steel plates. We can still do it when we try.'

'Let the dog see the rabbit,' said the porter as the lift stopped.

'This is six,' said Midgley.

'Every floor looks the same to me,' said his uncle.

'Did you ring our Hartley?' Hartley was Uncle Ernest's son and a chartered accountant.

'He's coming as soon as he can get away.'

'Was he tied up?'

He had been.

'Secretary was it? Was he in a meeting? I'd like to know what they are, these meetings he's always in, that he can't speak to his father. "Excuse me, I have to speak to my father." That's no disgrace, is it? "I won't be a moment, my dad's on the line." Who's going to take offence at that? Who are they, in these meetings? Don't they have fathers? I thought fathers were universal. Instead of which I have to make an appointment to see my own son. Sons, fathers, you shouldn't need appointments. You should get straight through. You weren't like that with your dad. Frank thought the world of you.'

They were going down the long corridor again.

'I came on the diesel,' said Uncle Ernest. He was lame in one leg.

'I go all over. I went to York last week. Saw the railway museum. There's stock in there I drove. Museum in my own lifetime. I'll tell you one thing.'

They stopped.

'What,' said Midgley.

'I wouldn't like to have to polish this floor.'

They resumed.

'You still schoolteaching?'

Midgley nodded.

47

'Pleased your dad, did that. Though it won't be much of a salary. You'd have been better off doing something in our Hartley's line. He's up there in the £30,000 bracket now. She was talking about a swimming pool.'

They stopped at the entrance to Intensive Care while his uncle stood, one arm stretched out to the wall, taking the weight off his leg.

'Is your Aunty Kitty here?'

'Yes.'

'I thought she would be. Where no vultures fly.'

Aunty Kitty got up and did her 'I am too upset to speak' act. 'Hello, Kitty,' said Ernest.

'I always thought I should be the first, Ernest.'

'Well you still might be. He's not dead yet.'

'Go in, Ernest.' She dabbed her nose. 'Go in.'

Uncle Ernest stood by his brother's bed. Then he sat down.

'This is summat fresh for you, Frank,' he said. 'You were always such a bouncer.' He stood up and leaned over the bed to look closer at the bleeps on the scanner. They were bouncing merrily. A nurse looked in.

'You're not to touch that.'

'I was just interested.'

'He's very ill.'

She paused for a moment, came further into the room and looked at the scanner. She looked at Uncle Ernest (though not, he noticed, at Frank) and went out.

'It's all mechanised now,' he said.

There was no sound in the room. The brothers had never had much to say to each other at the best of times. Without there being any animosity, they felt easier in the presence of a third party; alone they embarrassed each other. It was still the case, even though one of them was unconscious, and Uncle Ernest got up, thankful to be able to go.

'Ta-ra then, butt,' he said.

And waited.

He wanted to pat his brother's hand.

'I went to York last week,' he said. 'It hasn't changed much. They haven't spoiled it like they have Leeds. Though there's one of these precinct things. It's the first time I've been since we were lads. We went over on our bikes once.' Instead of touching his brother's hand he jogged his foot in farewell, just as the nurse was coming in.

'He's *very* ill,' she said, smoothing the coverlet over his brother's feet. 'And this is delicate equipment.'

'I went in,' she said in the canteen later, 'and there was one of them pulling a patient's leg about. He had hold of his foot. It's an uphill battle.'

Uncle Ernest's son Hartley came with his wife Jean and their children, Mark (14) and Elizabeth (10). Hartley hated hospitals, hence his demand for full family back-up. He was actually surprised that Mark had condescended to come: a big 14, Mark had long since passed beyond parental control and only appeared with the family on state occasions. The truth was that Miss Pollock, who took him for Religious Knowledge and who was known to be fucking at least one of the sixth form, had pointed out only last week how rare were the opportunities these days of seeing a dead person, and thus of acquiring a real perspective on the human condition. Mark was hoping this visit might gain him some status in the eyes of Miss Pollock. Sensitive to the realities of birth and death, he hoped to be the next candidate for 'bringing out'.

They were all going up in the lift.

'Think on,' said Hartley. 'It's quite likely your grandad'll be here. I don't want you asking for all sorts in front of him.'

'No,' said his wife. 'We don't want him saying you're spoiled.'

'Though you are spoiled,' said Hartley.

'Whose fault is that?' said Jean.

The steel doors folded back to reveal Denis saying goodbye to Uncle Ernest.

'Now then, Dad,' said Hartley. 'Hello, Denis. This is a bad do.'

Jean kissed the old man.

'Give your grandad a kiss, Elizabeth.'

The child did so.

'Come on, Mark.'

'I don't kiss now,' said the boy.

'You kiss your grandad,' said Hartley and the boy did so and a nurse, passing, looked.

'How is he?' said Hartley.

'Dying,' said his father. 'Sinking fast.'

'Oh dear, oh dear, oh dear,' said Hartley, who had hoped it would be all over by now.

'And how've you been keeping?' said Jean, brightly.

'Champion,' said Uncle Ernest. 'Is that one of them new watches?' He took Mark's wrist.

'He had to save up for it,' said Jean. 'You had to save up for it, didn't you, Mark?'

Mark nodded.

'He didn't,' said the little girl.

'I never had a watch till I was 21,' said the old man. 'Of course, they're 21 at 18 now, aren't they?'

Denis pressed the button for the lift.

'We'd better get along to the ward if he's that critical,' said Jean.

'I've had the receiver in my hand to give you a ring once or twice,' said Hartley as they waited for the lift, 'then a client's come in.'

'I was thinking of going to Barnard Castle next week,' said Ernest.

'Whatever for?' said Jean, kissing him goodbye.

'I've never been.' He shook Denis's hand. The lift doors closed. Hartley and his family walked ahead of Midgley down the long corridor.

'I'll give you such a clatter when I get you home, young lady,' Jean was saying. 'He did save up.'

'Only a week,' said the child.

'When we get there,' said Hartley, 'We want to go in in twos. All together would be too much of a strain.'

'What's he doing going to Barnard Castle?' said Jean.

'He can't be short of money taking himself off to Barnard Castle.'

Midgley caught them up.

'You'd no need all to come,' he said. 'I wouldn't let Joyce bring ours.'

'They wanted to come,' said Jean. 'Our Mark

did especially, didn't you Mark?'

'It's more handy for us, anyway,' said Hartley. 'What did we do before the M62?'

Mark was disappointed. The old man was quite plainly breathing. He could quite easily have been asleep. He wasn't even white.

'He's not my uncle, is he, Dad?'

'He's my uncle. He's your great-uncle.'

Hartley was looking at the screen.

'You see this screen, Mark? It's monitoring his heartbeats.'

Mark didn't look, but said wearily, 'I know, Dad.'

'I was only telling you.'

Hartley touched the screen where the beep was flickering.

'You want to learn, don't you?' his father said as they came out.

'Dad.' The boy stopped. 'We made one of those at school.'

Jean now led little Elizabeth in. ('Bless her,' said Aunty Kitty.)

They stood hand in hand by the bedside, and

Jean bent down and kissed him.

'Do you want me to kiss him?' said the child.

'No. I don't think so, love,' and she rubbed her lips with her hanky where they had touched him.

'Are you crying, Mam?' said the child.

'Yes.'

The little girl looked up at her.

'There aren't any tears.'

'You can cry without tears,' said her mother, looking at the monitor. 'You can cry more without tears.'

'I can't,' said the child. 'How do you do it, Mam?'

'It comes when you're grown up.'

'I want to be able to do it now.'

'Listen, I'll give you such a smack in a minute,' said her mother. 'He's dying.'

Elizabeth began to cry.

'There, love.' Her mother hugged her. 'He doesn't feel it.'

'I'm not crying because of him,' said the child. 'I'm crying because of you.'

'I wouldn't have another Cortina,' said Hartley. 'I used to swear by Cortinas. No longer.'

Midgley was watching an Indian man and his son sat in the corner. The father's face ran with tears as he hugged the child to him so that he seemed in danger of smothering the boy.

'You still got the VW?'

Midgley nodded.

'I think I might go in for a Peugeot,' said Hartley. 'A 604. Buy British.' There was a pause, and he added: 'He was a nice old chap.'

Jean and Elizabeth returned and Mark, who had been in the corridor, came in to ask how long they were stopping.

Hartley looked at Jean.

'I think we ought to wait just a bit, don't you, darling?'

'Oh yes,' said Jean. 'Just in case.'

Aunty Kitty came in. 'I've just had one coffee and a wagon wheel and it was 45p. And it's all supposed to be voluntary.'

'There isn't a disco, is there?' said Mark.

'Disco?' said Jean. 'Disco? This is a hospital.'

'Well. Leisure facilities. Facilities for visitors.

Killing time.'

'Listen,' Jean hissed. 'Your Uncle Denis's father is dying and you talk about discos.'

'It's all right,' said Midgley.

'Here, go get yourself a coffee,' said Hartley, giving him a pound. Aunty Kitty looked away.

Hartley and his family were going. They were congregated outside the lift.

'You'll wait, I expect,' said Hartley.

'Oh yes,' said Midgley, 'I want to be here.'

'You want to make it plain at this stage you don't want him resuscitating.'

'That's if he doesn't want him resuscitating,' said Jean. 'You don't know.'

'I wouldn't want my dad resuscitating,' said Hartley.

'Denis might, mightn't you Denis?'

'No,' said Midgley.

'You often don't get the choice,' said Hartley. 'They'll resuscitate anybody given half a chance. Shove them on these life-support machines. It's all to do with cost-effectiveness. They invest in this expensive equipment then they feel they have to use it.' He pumped the lift button. 'My guess is that it'll be at four in the morning, the crucial time. That's when life's at its lowest ebb, the early hours.'

'Miracles do happen, of course,' said Jean. 'I was reading about these out-of-body experiences. Have you read about them, Denis? It's where very sick people float in the air above their own bodies. Personally,' Jean kissed Midgley, 'I think it won't be long before science will be coming round to an after-life. Bye bye. I wish it had been on a happier occasion.'

Midgley went down the long corridor.

'Money's no good,' said Aunty Kitty. 'Look at President Kennedy. They've been a tragic family.'

The Indians slept, the little son laid with his head in the father's lap.

An orderly came in and tidied the magazines, emptied the waste-bin and took away a vase of flowers.

'Oxygen,' he said as he went out.

'The Collingwoods got back from Corfu,' said Aunty Kitty. 'They said they enjoyed it but they wouldn't go a second time.'

It was after ten and Midgley had assumed she was going to stay the night when she suddenly got up.

'If I go now I can get the twenty-to,' she said. 'I'll just get back before they're turning out. I never go upstairs. It's just asking for it.'

'I'll walk down with you,' said Midgley.

She tiptoed elaborately past the sleeping immigrants, favouring them with a benevolent smile.

'They've got feelings the same as us,' she whispered. 'They're fond of their families. More so, probably.' They came out into the corridor. 'But then they're less advanced than we are.'

He phoned Joyce.

She and Colin were watching a programme about dolphins that had been introduced by the Duke of Edinburgh. Her mother was asleep with her mouth open.

'What're you doing?' asked Midgley.

'Nothing. Colin's watching a programme about dolphins. How is he?'

Midgley told her.

'I've got to stay,' he finished.

'Why? You've done all that's necessary. Nobody's going to blame you.'

Midgley saw that somebody had written on the wall 'Pray for me.' A wag had added 'OK.'

'I must be here when he goes,' said Midgley. 'You can understand that.'

'I understand you,' she said. 'It's not love. It's not affection.' Colin looked up. 'It's yourself.'

She put the phone down.

'Dad?' said Colin.

She turned the television off. 'He's hanging on.'

'Who?'

'Your grandad.' She got up. 'Wake up Mother. Time for bed.'

Midgley went back and sat with his father. While he had been out the night nurse had come on. She was a plump girl, dark, less pert than the others,

60

and, he thought, more human. Actually she was just dirty. The hair wasn't gathered properly under her cap and there was a ladder in her stocking. She straightened the bedclothes, bending over the inert form so that her behind was inches from Midgley's face. Midgley decided it wasn't deliberate.

'Am I in the way?' he asked.

'No,' she said. 'Why? Stop there.'

She looked at the television monitor for a minute or two, counting the jumps with her watch. Then she smiled and went out. Five minutes later she was back with a cup of tea.

'No sugar,' said Midgley.

'May I?' she said and put both lumps in her mouth.

'Slack tonight,' she said. 'Still it just needs one drunken driver.'

Midgley closed his eyes.

'I thought you were going to be a bit of company,' she said. 'You're tired out.' She fetched a pillow and they went out into the waiting room. The Indians had gone.

'Lie down,' she said. 'I'll wake you if anything happens.'

Around five an alarm went off, and there were two deaths in quick succession. Midgley slept on. At eight he woke.

'You can't lie down,' said a voice. 'You're not supposed to lie down.' It was a clean, fresh nurse.

Two women he had not seen before sat watching him.

'The nurse said she'd wake me up.'

'What nurse?'

'If anything happened to my father.'

'Whose is that pillow?'

'Midgley. Mr Midgley.'

'It's a hospital pillow.' She took it, and went back inside to her desk.

'Midgley.' Her finger ran down the list. 'No change. But don't lie down. It's not fair on other people.'

Midgley went and looked at his father. No change was right. He felt old and dirty. He had not shaved and there was a cold sore starting on his lip. But with his father there was no change.

Still clean. Still pink. Still breathing. The dot skipped on. He walked out to the car park where he had left his van and wondered if he dared risk going out to buy a razor.

He went back in search of the doctor.

He cut across the visitors' car park, empty now except for his van, and took a path round the outside of the hospital that he thought would take him round to the entrance. The buildings were long and low and set in the hillside. They were done in identical units, every ward the same. He was passing a ward that seemed just like his father's except where his father should have been a woman was just putting her breast to a baby's mouth. A nurse came to the window and stared at him. He looked away hurriedly and walked on, but not so quickly as to leave her with the impression he had been watching. She was still staring at him as he turned the corner. He experienced a feeling of relief if not quite homecoming when he saw he was now outside Intensive Care. He picked out his father's room, saw the carnations on the window sill and the head and shoulders of a nurse. She was obviously looking at the bed. She moved back towards the window to make room for someone else. Midgley stood on tiptoe to try and see what was happening. He thought there was someone else there in a white coat. The room was full of people.

Midgley ran round the unit trying to find a way in. There was a door at the end of the building with an empty corridor beyond. It was locked. He ran up to the path again, then cut down across the bank through some young trees to try another door. A man on the telephone watched him sliding down then put one phone down and picked up another. Midgley ran on and suddenly was in a muddy flower bed among bushes and evergreens. It was the garden around the entrance to the Reception Area. Upstairs he ran past the startled nurse at the desk and into his father's room. Nobody spoke. There was an atmosphere of reverence.

'Is he dead?' said Midgley. 'Has he gone?' He was panting. An older woman in blue turned round. 'Dead? Certainly not. I am the matron.

And look at your shoes.'

Behind the matron Midgley caught a glimpse of his father. As a nurse bustled him out Midgley struggled to look back. He was sure his father was smiling.

'I've just been to spend a penny,' said Aunty Kitty. 'When you consider it's a hospital the toilets are nothing to write home about. Look at your shoes.'

She was beginning to settle in, had brought a flask, sandwiches, knitting.

'I know Frank,' she said, looking at *Country Life*. 'He'll make a fight of it. I wouldn't thank you for a place in Bermuda.'

Midgley went to the gents to have a wash. He got some toilet paper and stood by the basins wiping the mud off his boots. He was stood with the muddy paper in his hands when an orderly came in, looked at the paper then looked at him incredulously, shook his head and went into a cubicle saying: 'The fucking public. The fucking dirty bastard public.'

Midgley went down to ring his Uncle Ernest on

the phone outside physio. A youngish woman was just dialling.

'Cyril. It's . . .' She held the mouthpiece away from her mouth and the earpiece from her ear. 'It's Vi. Vi. I am speaking into it. Mum's had her op. No. She's had it. Had it this morning first thing. She's not come round yet, but I spoke to the sister and apparently she's fine. FINE. And the sister says . . .' She dropped her voice. 'It wasn't what we thought. It wasn't what we thought. No. So there's no need to worry.' She ran her finger over the acoustic headboard behind the phone, fingering the holes. 'No. Completely clear. Well I think it's good news, don't you? The sister said the surgeon is the best. Mr Caldecott. People pay thousands to have him. Anyway I'm so relieved. Aren't you? Yes. Bye.'

As Midgley took the phone she took out her handkerchief and rubbed it over her lips, and safely outside the hospital, her ear.

Uncle Ernest had said on the phone that if this was going to go on he wasn't sure he could run to the fares, but he turned up in the late afternoon along with Hartley.

He went and sat with his brother for a bit, got down and looked under the bed and figured out how the mechanism worked that lifted and lowered it and finally stood up and said, 'Gillo, Frank,' which was what he used to say when they went out cycling between the wars. It meant 'hurry up'.

'It's Frank all over,' said Aunty Kitty, 'going down fighting. He loved life.'

There were a couple of newcomers in the waiting room, an oldish couple.

'It's their eldest daughter,' whispered Aunty Kitty. 'She was just choosing some new curtains in Schofields. Collapsed. Suspected brain haemorrhage. Their other son's a vet.'

They trailed down the long corridor to the lift.

'It's a wonder to me,' said Uncle Ernest, 'how your Aunty Kitty's managed to escape strangulation all these years. Was he coloured, this doctor?'

'Which?' said Midgley.

'That said he was on his last legs.'

Midgley reluctantly admitted he was.

'That explains it,' said the old railwayman.

'Dad,' said Hartley.

'What does that mean, "Dad"?' said his father.

'It means I'm vice-chairman of the community relations council. It means we've got one in the office and he's a tip-top accountant. It means we all have to live with one another in this world.' He pumped the button of the lift.

'I'll not come again,' said Uncle Ernest. 'It gets morbid.'

'We've just got to play it by ear,' said Hartley.

'You won't have this performance with me,' said the old man. 'Come once and have done.'

'Shall I drop you?' said Hartley as the doors opened.

'I don't want you to go out of your way.'

'No, but shall I drop you?'

'Press G,' said Uncle Ernest.

The lift doors closed.

Midgley was sitting with his father when the

plump night nurse came on.

'I wondered if you'd be on tonight.' He read her tab. 'Nurse Lightfoot.'

'Waiting for me, were you? No change.' She took a tissue and wiped the old man's mouth. 'He doesn't want to leave us, does he?' She picked up the vase of carnations from the window sill. 'Oxygen,' she said and took them outside.

Later, when she had made him a cup of tea and Aunty Kitty had gone home for the second night, he was sitting at the bedside but got up when she started to give his father a bed bath.

'You're like one another.'

He stared out of the window, even moved to avoid seeing the reflection.

'No,' he said.

'You are. It's a compliment. He has a nice face.' She sponged under his arms.

'What are you?' she said.

'How do you mean?' He turned just as she had folded back the sheets and was sponging between his legs. Quickly he looked out of the window again.

69

'What do you do?'

'Teacher. I'm a teacher.' He wanted to go and sit in the waiting room.

'What was he?'

'Plumber.'

'He's got lovely hands. Real ladies' hands.'

And it was true. She had finished and the soft white hands of his father lay over the sheet.

'That happens in hospitals. People's hands change.' She held his father's hand. Midgley wondered if he could ask her to hold his. Probably. She looked even more of a mess than the night before.

'Is there anything you want to ask?'

'Yes,' said Midgley.

'If there is, doctor'll be round in a bit.'

It was a different doctor. Not Indian. Fair, curly-haired and aged not much more than fourteen.

'His condition certainly hasn't deteriorated,' the child said. 'On the other hand,' he glanced boyishly at the chart, 'it can't be said to have improved.'

Midgley wondered if he had ever had his ears pierced.

'I don't know that there's any special point in waiting. You've done your duty.' He gave him a winning smile and had Midgley been standing closer would probably have put his hand on his arm as he had been taught to do.

'After all,' he was almost conspiratorial, 'he doesn't know you're here.'

'I don't think he's dying,' said Midgley.

'Living, dying,' said the boy and shrugged. The words meant the same thing.

'You do want your father to live?' He turned towards the nurse and pulled a little face.

'I was told he wasn't going to last long. I live in Hull.'

'Our task is to make them last as long as possible.' The pretty boy looked at his watch. 'We've no obligation to get them off on time.'

'Some of them seem to think we're British Rail,' the doctor remarked to a nurse in the small hours when they were having a smoke after sexual intercourse.

'I don't like 15-year-old doctors, that's all,' said Midgley. 'I'm old enough to be his father. Does nobody else wait? Does nobody else feel they have to be here?'

'Why not go sleep in your van? I can give you a pillow and things.' She was eating a toffee. 'I'll send somebody down to the car park if anything happens.'

'What do you do all day?' asked Midgley.

'Sleep.' She was picking a bit of toffee from her tooth. 'I generally surface around three.'

'Maybe we could have a coffee. If he's unchanged.'

'OK.'

She smiled. He had forgotten how easy it was.

'I'll just have another squint at my dad.'

He came back. 'Come and look. I think he's moved.'

She ran ahead of him into the room. The old man lay back on the pillows, a shaded light by the bed.

'You had me worried for a moment,' she said. 'It's all right.'

'No. His face has changed.'

She switched on the lamp over the bed, the light so sudden and bright that that alone might have made the old man flinch. But nothing moved.

'It's just that he seemed to be smiling.'

'You're tired,' she said, put her hand against his face and switched out the light.

Midgley switched it on again.

'If you look long enough at him you'll see a smile.'

'If you look long enough,' she said, walking out of the room, 'you'll see anything you want.'

Midgley stood for a moment in the darkened room, wishing he had kissed her when he'd had the chance. He went out to look for her but there had been a pile-up on the M62 and all hell was about to break loose.

'What do you do all day?' said his wife on the phone. 'Sit in the waiting room. Sit in his room. Walk round the hospital.'

'Don't they mind?'

'Not if they're going to die.'

'Is he, though?' said his wife, watching her mother who had taken up her station on the chair by the door, holding her bag on her knees, preparatory to going to bed. 'It seems a long time.' The old lady was falling asleep. Once she had slipped right off that chair and cracked her head on the sideboard. That had been a hospital do.

'I can't talk. Mum's waiting to go up. She's crying out for a bath. I'm just going to have to steel myself.' The handbag slipped to the floor.

'I need a bath,' said Midgley.

'Go over to your dad's,' said his wife. 'Mum's falling over. Bye.'

'What am I doing sat on this seat?' said her mother, as she got her up. 'I never sit on this seat. I don't think I've ever sat on this seat before.'

In the morning Midgley was woken by Nurse Lightfoot banging on the steamed-up window of the van. It was seven o'clock.

'I'm just going off,' she was mouthing

through the glass.

He wound down the window.

'I'm just coming off. Isn't it a grand morning? I'm going to have a big fried breakfast then go to bed. I'll see you at teatime. You look terrible.'

Midgley looked at himself in the driving mirror, then started up the van and drove after her, hooting.

'You're not supposed to hoot,' she said. 'It's a hospital.'

'I forgot to ask you. How's my dad?'

'No change.' She waved and ran down a grass bank towards the nurses' flats. 'No change.'

His dad lived where he had lived once, at the end of a terrace of redbrick back-to-back houses. It was an end house, as his mother had always been careful to point out. It gave them one more window, which was nice, only kids used the end wall to play football against, which wasn't. His dad used to heave himself up from the fireside and go out to them, night after night. He let himself in with the key he had had since he was 14. 'You're 21 now,' his mother had said.

The house was neat and clean and cold. He looked for some sign of interrupted activity, even a chair out of place, some clue as to what his father had been doing when the blow fell. But there was nothing. He had a home help. She had probably tidied up. He put the kettle on, before having a shave. He knew where everything was. His dad's razor on the shelf above the sink, a shaving brush worn down to a stub and a half-used packet of Seven O'Clock blades. He scrubbed away the caked rust from the razor ('Your dad doesn't care,' said his mother) and put in a new blade. He had never gone in for shaving soap. Puritan soap they always bought, green Puritan soap. Then having shaved he took his shirt off to wash in the same sequence he had seen his father follow every night when he came in from work. Then, thinking of the coming afternoon, he did something he had never seen his father do, take off his trousers and his pants to wash his cock. He smelled his shirt. It stank. Naked, white and shivering he went through the neat sitting room and up the narrow stairs and stood on the cold lino of his parents' bedroom looking at himself in the dressing-table mirror. On top of the dressing-table, stood on little lace mats, was a toilet set. A round glass jar for a powder-puff, a pin tray, a cut-glass dish with a small pinnacle in the middle, for rings, and a celluloid-backed mirror and hair-brush. Items that had never had a practical use, but which had lain there in their appointed place for forty years.

He opened the dressing-table drawer, and found a new shirt still in its packet. They had given it to his father as a Christmas present two years before. He put it on, carefully extracting all the pins and putting them in the cut-glass dish. He looked for pants and found a pair that were old, baggy and gone a bit yellow. Some socks. Nothing quite fitted. He was smaller than his father. These days it was generally the other way round. He went downstairs, through into the scullery to polish his shoes. He remembered the brushes, the little brush to put the polish on which as a child he had always thought of as bad, the big noble brush that brought out the shine. He stood on the hearthrug and saw himself in the mirror, ready as if for a funeral, and sat down on the settee about to weep when he realised it was not his father's funeral he was imagining but his own. On the end of the tiled mantelpiece of which his mother had been so proud when they had had it put in in 1953 (a crime getting rid of that beautiful range, Joyce always said) was his dad's pipe. It was still half full of charred tobacco. He put it back but rolling over it fell on to the hearth. He stooped to pick it up and was his father suddenly, bending down, falling and lying there two days with the pipe under his hand. He dashed out of the house and drove wildly back to the hospital.

'No change,' said the nurse wearily (they were beginning to think he was mad). But if there was no change at least the old man didn't seem to be smiling.

'I'm wearing your shirt, Dad,' Midgley said. 'The one we gave you for Christmas. I hope that's all right. It doesn't really suit me, but I think that's why Joyce bought it. She said it didn't suit me but it would suit you.'

A nurse came in.

'They tell you to talk,' said Midgley. 'I read it in an article in the *Reader's Digest*,' (and as if this gave it added force), 'it was in the waiting room.'

The nurse sniffed. 'They say the same thing about plants,' she said, putting the carnations back on the window sill. 'I think it's got past that stage.'

Midgley was sitting on the divan bed in Nurse Lightfoot's room in the nurses' quarters. The rooms were light and modern like the hospital. She was sitting by the electric fire with one bar on. There was a Snoopy poster on the wall.

'People are funny about nurses,' she said. 'Men.' She took a bite of her bun. They were muesli buns. 'You say you're a nurse and their whole attitude changes. Do you know what I mean?'

'No,' lied Midgley.

'I notice it at parties particularly. They ask you what you do, you say you're a nurse and next minute they've got you on the floor. Perfectly ordinary people turn into wild beasts.' She switched another bar on.

'I've given up saying I'm a nurse for that reason.'

'What do you say you are?' asked Midgley. He wondered whether he would be better placed if he went over to the fire or he got her to come over to the bed.

'I say I'm a sales representative. I don't mean you,' she said. 'You're obviously not like that. Course you've got other things on your mind at the moment.'

'Like what?'

'Your dad.'

'Oh yes.'

The duty nurse had been instructed to ring if there was any sign of a crisis.

'He is lovely,' she said, through mouthfuls of bun. 'I do understand the way you feel about him.'

'Do you?' said Midgley. 'That's nice.'

'Old people have their own particular attraction. He's almost sexy.'

Midgley stood up suddenly.

She picked something out of her mouth.

'Was your cake gritty?'

'No,' said Midgley, sitting down again.

'Mine was. Mine was a bit gritty.'

'It was probably meant to be gritty,' said Midgley, looking at his watch.

'No. It was more gritty than that.'

'What would you say,' asked Midgley, as he carefully examined a small stain on the bedcover, 'what would you say if I asked you to go to bed.'

'Now?' she asked, extracting another piece of grit or grain.

'If you like.' He made it sound as if she had made the suggestion.

'I can't now.' She gathered up the cups and plates.

'Why not? You're not on till seven.'

'It's Wednesday. I'm on early turn.' She wondered if he was going to turn into a wild beast.

'Tomorrow then?'

'Tomorrow would be better. Though of course it all depends.'

'What on?'

She was shocked.

'Your father. He may not be here tomorrow.'

'That's true,' said Midgley, getting up. He kissed her fairly formally.

'Anyway,' she smiled. 'Fingers crossed.'

Midgley sat by his father's bed and watched the dot skipping on the screen.

'Hold on, Dad,' he muttered. 'Hold on.'

There was no change.

Before going down to sleep in the van he telephoned home. It was his son who answered. Joyce was upstairs with her mother.

'Could you ask her to come to the phone, please,' said Midgley. The 'please' was somehow insulting. He heard brief shouting.

'She can't,' said Colin. 'Gran's in the bath. Mum can't leave her. What do you want?'

'You go up and watch her while I speak to your Mum.'

'Dad.' The boy's voice was slow with weary outrage. 'Dad. She's in the bath. She's no clothes on. I don't want to see her.'

He heard more distant shouting.

'Mum says if she can get a granny-sitter she may come over to see Grandad.'

'Colin.' Midgley was suddenly urgent. 'Colin. Are you still there?'

'Sure.' (Midgley hated that.)

'Tell her not to do that. Do you hear? Tell her there's no need to come over. Go on, tell her.'

'I'll tell her when she comes down.'

'No,' said Midgley. 'Now. I know you. Go up and tell her now.'

The phone was put down and he could hear Colin bellowing up the stairs. He came back.

'I told her. Is that all?'

'No,' said Midgley. 'Haven't you forgotten something? How's Grandad? Haven't you forgotten that? Well it's nice of you to ask, Colin. He's about the same, Colin, thank you.'

'How was your grandad?' said Joyce, coming downstairs with a wet towel and a bundle of her mother's underclothes.

'About the same,' said Colin.

'And your dad?'

'No change.'

That night Midgley dreamed it was morning when the door opened and his father got into the van.

'I didn't know you drove, Dad,' he said as they were going into town. 'When did you learn?'

'Just before I died.'

His mother, as a girl, met them outside the Town Hall.

'What a spanking van, Frank,' she said. 'Move up, Denis, let me sit next to your dad.'

The three of them sat in a row until he saw her hand was on his father's leg, when suddenly he was in a field alone with his mother.

'What a grand field,' she said. 'It's spotless.'

He was a little boy and she was in a white frock, and some terrible threat had just been lifted. Then he looked behind him and saw something much worse. On the edge of the field, ready to engulf them, was an enormous slag heap, glinting black and shiny in the sun. His mother hadn't seen it and chattered on how lovely this field was and slipping nearer came this terrible hill. Someone ran down the slope, waving his arms, a figure big and filthy, a miner, a coalman. He slid down beside them.

'Oh,' she said placidly, 'here's your father,' and he sat down beside her, coal and muck all over her white frock.

Then they were walking through Leeds Market. It was Sunday and the stalls were empty and shuttered. It was also a church and they walked up through the market to the choir screen. It was in the form of a board announcing Arrivals and Departures, slips of board clicking over with names on them, only instead of Arrivals and Departures it was headed Births and Deaths. Midgley wandered off while his parents sat looking at the board. Then his mam got up and kissed his dad, and went backwards through the screen just before the gates were drawn across. Midgley tried to run down the church and couldn't. He was shouting 'Mam. Mam.' Eventually he got to the gates and started shaking them, but she had gone. He turned to look at his father who shook his head slowly and turned away. Midgley went on rattling the gates then someone was shaking the van. It was Nurse Lightfoot waking him up. 'You can call me Valery,' she chanted as she ran off to her big breakfast.

Later that morning Midgley went in to see his father to find a smartish middle-aged woman sat by the bed. She was holding his father's hand.

'Is it Denis?' she said without getting up.

'Yes.'

'I'm Alice Dugdale. Did he tell you about me?'

'No.'

'He wouldn't, being him. He's an old bugger. Aren't you?'

She shook the inert hand. She was in her fifties, Midgley decided, very confident and done up to the nines. His mother would have called her common. She looked like the wife of a prosperous licensee.

'He told me about you,' she said. 'He never stopped telling me about you. It's a sad sight.'

The nurse had said his father was a bit better

this morning.

'His condition's stabilised,' said Midgley.

'Yes, she said that to me, the little slut. What does she know?' She looked at him. 'You're a bit scruffy.' She stood up and smoothed down her skirt. 'I've come from Southport.' She took the carnations from the vase and put them in the waste-bin. 'A depressing flower, carnations,' she said. 'I prefer freesias. I'm a widow,' she said. 'A rich widow. Shall we have a meander round? No sense in stopping here.' She kissed his father on the forehead. 'His lordship's not got much to contribute. Bye bye chick.'

She swept through the waiting room with Midgley in her wake. Aunty Kitty open-mouthed got up and went out to watch them going down the corridor.

'That'll be your Aunty Kitty, I take it.' She said it loudly enough for her to hear.

'It is, yes,' said Denis, glancing back and smiling weakly. 'Do you know her?'

'No, thank God. Though she probably knows me.'

They found a machine and had some coffee. She took a silver flask from her bag.

'Do you want some of this in it?'

'No thanks,' said Midgley.

'I'd better,' she said. 'I've driven from Southport. I wanted to marry your dad only he said no. I had too much money. My husband left me very nicely placed. He was a leading light in the soft furnishing trade. Frank would have felt beholden, you see. That was your dad all over. Still you know what he was like.'

Midgley was no longer sure he did.

'How do you mean?' he said.

'He always had to be the one, did Frank. The one who did the good turns, the one who paid out, the one who sacrificed. You couldn't do anything for him. I had all this money and he wouldn't even let me take him to Scarborough. We used to go sit in Roundhay Park. Roundhay Park!'

A woman went by, learning to use crutches.

'We could have been in Tenerife.'

Midgley was glad to have at least this aspect of his father's character confirmed.

'I didn't want to let him down,' said Midgley. 'That's why I've been waiting. He wants me to let him down, I know.'

'Poor soul,' she said, looking at the woman struggling down the corridor.

'What was your mam like?'

'She was lovely,' said Midgley.

'She must have had him taped. She looks a grand woman. He's showed me photographs.' She took out her compact and made up her face. 'I'll go back and have another look. Then I've got to get over to a Round Table in Harrogate. Killed two birds with one stone for me, this trip.'

'Your mother'd not been dead a year,' sniffed Aunty Kitty. 'I was shocked.'

'I'm not shocked.'

'You're a man.'

'It wasn't like your dad. She's a cheek showing her face.'

'I'm rather pleased,' said Midgley.

'That hair's dyed,' said Aunty Kitty, but it was a last despairing throw. 'They're sending him downstairs tomorrow. He must be on the mend.' The drama was about to go out of her life. 'I only hope when he does come round he's not a veg-etable.'

'I've told Shirley to ring if anything happens,' Valery said. 'Not that it will. His chest is better. His heart is better. He's simply unconscious now.'

Midgley was brushing his teeth.

'I'm looking forward to him coming round.' She raised her voice above the running tap. 'I long to know what his voice is like.'

'What?' said Midgley turning off the tap.

'I long to know what his voice is like.'

'Oh,' said Midgley. 'Yes.' And turned the tap on again.

'I think I know what it's like,' she said. 'I'd just like to have it confirmed.'

'You don't seem to like talking about your father,' she said as she unzipped her skirt. 'Nice shirt.'

'Yes,' said Midgley. 'It's one of Dad's.'

'I like it.'

He went and had a pee and while he was out she took the receiver off the phone and put a cushion over it. When he came back she was already in bed.

'Hello,' he said, getting in and lying beside her. 'It's a bit daft is this.'

'Why?' she said. 'It happens all the time.'

'Yes,' said Midgley. 'So I'm told.'

They kissed.

'I ought to have done more of this.'

'What?'

'This,' said Midgley. 'This is going to be the rule from now on. I've got a lot of catching up to do.'

He ran his hand between her thighs.

'It's the nick of time.'

'First time I've heard it called that.'

'I hope this isn't one of those private beds,' said Midgley. 'I'm opposed to that on principle.'

'You've never asked me if I was married,' she said.

'You're a nurse. That puts you in a different

category.' There was a pause. 'Are you married?'

'He's on an oil rig.'

'I hope so,' said Midgley.

Later on he had a cigarette and she had a cake.

'I was certain they were going to ring from the ward,' he said.

'No.' She lifted up the cushion and put the receiver back.

He frowned. Then grinned. 'No harm done,' he said.

They were just settling in again when the phone rang. She answered.

'Yes,' she said, looking at him. 'Yes.'

'What's the matter?' said Midgley.

She put the phone down and looked away.

He was already out of bed and pulling his trousers on.

'Had she rung before?'

She had turned to face the wall.

'Had she?' Midgley was shouting. 'Was she ringing?'

'Don't shout. There are night nurses asleep.'

At the end of the long corridor the doors burst open.

'It's the biggest wonder I'd not gone into see Mrs Tunnicliffe,' said Aunty Kitty. 'She's in Ward 7 with her hip. She's been waiting two years. But I don't know what it was. Something made me come back upstairs. I was sat looking at a *Woman's Own* then in walks Joyce and next minute the nurse is calling us in and he has his eyes open! So we were both there, weren't we.'

Mrs Midgley nodded. They were all three stood by the bedside.

'He just said, "Is our Denis here? Is our Denis here?"' said Aunty Kitty, 'and I said: "He's just coming, Frank." And he smiled a little smile and it was all over. Bless him. I was his only sister.'

The body lay flat on the bed, the eyes closed, the sheet up to the neck.

'The dot does something different when you're dying,' said Aunty Kitty, looking at the screen which now showed a continuous line. 'I wasn't watching it, naturally, but I noticed out of the corner of my eye it was doing something different during the last moments.'

'I think he's smiling,' said Mrs Midgley.

'Of course he's smiling,' said Midgley. He went and looked out of the window. 'He's won. Scored. In the last minute of extra time.'

Mrs Midgley came over to the window and said in an undertone: 'You disgust me.'

A nurse came in and switched off the monitor. They went out.

'It's a pity you weren't here, Denis,' said Aunty Kitty. 'I mean when it came to the crunch. You've been so good. You've been here all the time he was dying. What were you doing?'

'Living,' said Midgley.

'He's at peace anyway,' said Aunty Kitty.

They went out and got his clothes. As they were walking out a young man was on the phone. 'It's a boy!' he was saying. 'A boy! Yes. Just think. I'm a father.'

They stood in the car park.

'I suppose while we're here,' said Joyce, 'we could go up home and make a start on going through his things.'

Father! Father! Burning Bright *was first published* in the London Review of Books. The London Review of Books *may be ordered through your local newsagent or taken on subscription. For subscriptions please call* 020 7209 1141 *or fax* 020 7209 1151